FOREST

BY BRENDAN KEARNEY

"Land ahoy!" Finn shouted to Skip, as he rowed eagerly towards the shore. "Let our adventure begin, old boy!"

Finn dragged the boat up the beach,

prepared the bike for the first
part of their adventure,

and stopped for a quick snack. "I'll save
some of these for later," Finn said,
as he packed some guavas
into his backpack.

Then they set off, cycling past vast lakes,

over tall mountains,

and into thick, lush rainforest –
where they found a river
to row along.

"This is amazing!" Finn shouted over the sound of rushing water, as they paddled deeper into the forest.

"There is life wherever you look!"

Wheeeeeeeeee!

There were birds and butterflies in the canopy.

There were many animals living among the trees.

And the undergrowth was full of creepy-crawlies!

But suddenly, there were no more trees and the animals were gone.

"This isn't right!" Finn cried.
"Why have all the trees been cut down?"

As they stood scratching their heads, a young tapir
spotted their backpack full of fruit.

And she looked very hungry.

"Here. Help yourself,"
Finn offered kindly.

"We can't leave her here all
alone, Skip. Let's stay with her
tonight and maybe her
parents will show up later."

As it got dark,

they pitched the tent,

collected some firewood,

and built a small campfire.

"We'll leave the tent open and perhaps your parents will arrive during the night," Finn suggested over dinner.

That night there were lots of visitors to the tent, but none of them were the little tapir's parents.

Soon the tent was full of animals looking for somewhere cosy to sleep.

In the morning, Finn handed out some breakfast
to the hungry animals. "I think the forest that once
stood here used to be their home," he said to Skip.

"We can't stay here," Finn turned to the
animals. "Skip and I will help you all
find a new part of the forest to live in."

They all climbed into Finn's boat
and off they set along the river.

But things didn't quite go to plan.

Finn could barely see where
he was going through the rain
and some strange, thick fog.

"Soon, Finn realised it wasn't fog.
"It's smoke!" he coughed.

They paddled quickly on.

"AHHHHHHH FIRE!"

Finn paddled as fast as he could,
past the smoke, flames,
and giant machines.

They rowed and rowed all day, and as the Sun
began to set they followed the sound of sirens
and the blinking of lights to some firefighters,
working hard to put out the flames.

The trees are being cut down and sold to make furniture, paper, and cardboard.

The stumps of trees and plants are burned away and cleared so that the land can be used for farming.

Or, the cleared land is used to grow palm trees to make palm oil - an ingredient in many types of food and other everyday things.

But we can help stop it!

Big changes start with small steps. Here are just some of the things you and Skip can do!

You can use less paper, and recycle or reuse things, so that fewer trees need to be chopped down.

If you can, try to buy things with an FSC logo. This means the wood used to make it was reused, or grown in a special forest where there is less damage to animals' homes.

FSC

You can also support charities that help to protect the environment.

Sounds like we can do our bit to help. And we can share what we've learned with others, too.

The following morning, they carried on down the river, until they found a luscious area in a protected part of the forest - where people made sure the trees weren't all burned down.

Even better - the tapir's parents
had made it here, too!

"Good luck in your new home,
everyone!" Finn called.

When Finn and Skip got home
they were more careful about
what they bought,

they used less paper and
recycled and reused more,

and they supported and helped
environmental charities
whenever they could.

They felt so pleased to be able to share what they had learned with others to help keep the rainforest a wonderful place.

WALK MORE

DRIVE LESS

SAVE OUR OCEANS

RECYCLE

WHAT CAN WE ALL DO?

BRENDAN KEARNEY

Brendan Kearney lives and works by the sea in South West England with his family and little dog, Crumble. He has loved drawing since he started scribbling as a child and feels very lucky to be able to draw for a living.

Finn and Skip are characters he has been drawing for years, and *Forest* is their second adventure after *Fish*. Brendan hopes they are able to help children understand some of the ecological issues facing our planet and give them a hopeful and productive way to play their part in making the world a better place.

Brendan loves pond dipping and fossil hunting, but absolutely hates carrots.

Penguin Random House

Produced for DK by Plum 5 Ltd

Editor Kathleen Teece
Designer Brandie Tully-Scott
Jacket Coordinator Issy Walsh
Production Editor Robert Dunn
Production Controller John Casey
Managing Editor Laura Gilbert
Managing Art Editor Diane Peyton Jones
Publishing Manager Francesca Young
Creative Director Mabel Chan
Publishing Director Sarah Larter

First published in Great Britain in 2022
by Dorling Kindersley Limited
DK, One Embassy Gardens, 8 Viaduct Gardens,
London, SW11 7BW
Copyright © 2021 Dorling Kindersley Limited
A Penguin Random House Company

10 9 8 7 6 5 4 3 2 1
001-323175-Jan/2022

A CIP catalogue record for this book
is available from the British Library.
ISBN: 978-0-2415-2579-1

Printed and bound in China

MIX
Paper from
responsible sources
FSC™ C018179

This book was made with Forest Stewardship
Council ™ certified paper - one small step in
DK's commitment to a sustainable future.
For more information go to
www.dk.com/our-green-pledge

For the curious
www.dk.com